Shopkins™

Once you shop...You can't stop!

Creativity Journal
by Jenne Simon

Scholastic Inc.

978-1-338-12750-8
10 9 8 7 6 5 4 3 2 1   17 18 19 20 21
Printed in Jiaxing, China
First printing, January 2017
Designed by Ben Mautner

Welcome to Shopville, where all your favorite Shopkins live, laugh, and savor the sweet things in life. Poppy Corn, Apple Blossom, Strawberry Kiss, and the rest of their friends have a world of fun in store for you in this journal. Inside these sweet and spicy pages, you can take quizzes, play games, write stories, and record all of your delicious adventures!

Check ya later!

AISLE BE SEEING YOU

Every aisle in the Small Mart is full of tasty surprises. But which aisle should you visit first? Take this quiz to find out!

What's your favorite weather?

A. Freezing snowfall
B. Crisp and cool
C. Hot like an oven
D. Pretty and clear

What kind of competition would you win?

A. Ice-skating
B. Pumpkin growing
C. Cake baking
D. Beauty pageant

How do you like to travel?

A. Cross-country ski
B. Banana boat
C. Submarine
D. Parade float

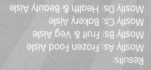

Results:
Mostly As: Frozen Food Aisle
Mostly Bs: Fruit & Veg Aisle
Mostly Cs: Bakery Aisle
Mostly Ds: Health & Beauty Aisle

PERFECT PAIRS

Whether you call them two peas in a pod or birds of a feather, these Shopkins complement each other like peanut butter and jelly. Draw a line between Shopkins from each column to match the Shopkins pairs that best go together.

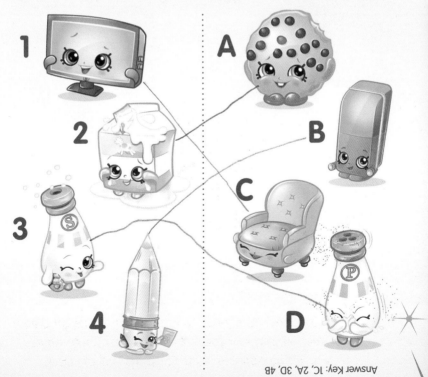

1

2

3

4

A

B

C

D

SELFIE PORTRAIT

All the Shopkins love saying "cheese" and snapping selfies. And now it's your turn! Draw a portrait of yourself in the empty photo frame. Soon your picture will be hanging in the Shopkins Hall of Fame!

DANCING IN THE AISLES

Can you match the Shopkins with their smoothest signature dance moves?

| worm | pop-and-lock | splits | bunny hop | cancan |

 1 Poppy Corn is the <u>pop-and-lock</u> queen of Shopville.

 2 Suzie Sundae sure is flexible. She can do the <u>Splits</u>.

 3 Drips likes to kick up his heels and do the <u>cancan</u>.

 4 Apple Blossom wriggles across the floor like a <u>worm</u>.

 5 Bun Bun Slipper gets everyone bouncing for the <u>bunny hop</u>.

CHILLY CHALLENGE

Oh, no! There's been an accident in the frozen food aisle, and everyone is mixed up. Can you unscramble the names of these cool Shopkins before they melt?

1. SPIPO OCOL <u>popsi cool</u>

2. CIE MCERA TAKE <u>ice cream cake</u>

3. YLIEK NOCE <u>Kylie cone</u>

4. OY-IHC <u>Yo-Chi</u>

5. ECI CMARE DMAER <u>ice cream dreamer</u>

Answer Key: 1. Popsi Cool 2. Ice Cream Kate 3. Kylie Cone 4. Yo-Chi 5. Ice Cream Dream

Chloe Flower

D'Lish Donut

Bread Head

Yo-Chi

Freda Fern

Mystery Shopkin

THE GREAT SHOPKINS SEARCH

Find the five Shopkins below in the word search puzzle. If you're an extra-seasoned detective, you'll find a mystery Shopkin hidden in the puzzle, too! Turn to the end of the book for the answers.

F R A T Q S C A N T
R M P O S C H A B O
E I D A F T L N O A
D L I S H D O N U T
A M B T G A E R I Y
F O P Y L S F B C S
E N Q P E U L P A E
R T S O R Y O C H I
N J A P F P W B A G
B R E A D H E A D I
F L U Q C E R T E N

PURR-FECT PETKINS

The Petkins are the furriest, friendliest, most loyal companions around. But which pet is purr-fect for you? Take this quiz to find out!

If you owned a business, what would it be?

A. A bookstore called The Wagging Tale
B. A gym called The Golden Scale
C. A nail salon called Claws and Paws

How do you like to spend Sunday mornings?

A. Playing at the park
B. Swimming laps
C. Napping on the couch

What's your weakness?

A. Barking up the wrong tree
B. Feeling like a fish out of water
C. The cat's got your tongue

Results:
Mostly As: Milk Bud
Mostly Bs: Fish Flake Jake
Mostly Cs: Hot Choc

SHOPPING CART RALLY

Which of the Shopkins is the fastest? They're having a race through the Small Mart to find out. Help Slick Breadstick, Poppy Corn, and Waffle Sue find the quickest way to the finish line! Turn to the end of the book for the answer key.

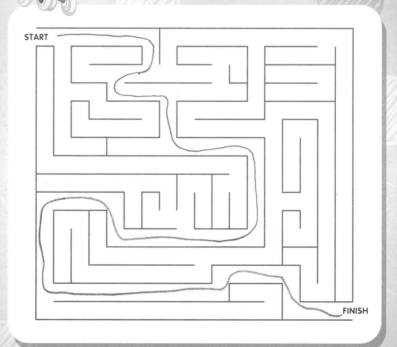

START

FINISH

BEST BIRTHDAY EVER

How old will you be on your next birthday? Draw the correct number of candles on top of Wishes—and then color and add in any extra delicious toppings you would want on your dream birthday cake!

TODAY'S SPECIAL

There are lots of things that make each of the Shopkins special. Look at the pictures below, and see if you can spot the differences.

FASHION FEVER

Lippy Lips is in the market for new accessories. She wants to leave her mark on Shopville's style scene. Draw the items that you think will help this colorful fashionista shine!

THE PRODUCE PUZZLE

The Shopkins in the Fruit & Veg aisle have taken a tumble and gotten scrambled. Can you rearrange the names of these fresh Shopkins and help sort them out?

1. PELNAPIPE SHRUC _Pineapple crush_

2. SIMS SHUMY OOM _miss mushy moo_

3. TWESE APE _Sweet pea_

4. CHEPAY _Peachy_

WHICH SHOPKIN ARE YOU?

The Shopkins are a wild bunch. Each one is full of flavor and bursting with personality. Which one are you most like? Take this personality quiz to find your Shopkin twin!

What's your favorite activity?

- **A.** Shopping and makeovers
- **B.** Skimming a magazine
- **C.** Snickering and doodling
- **D.** Toasting your friends

What's your pet peeve?

- **A.** Clashing colors
- **B.** When movie endings are spoiled
- **C.** Stale jokes
- **D.** Getting buttered up

What's your motto?

- **A.** "Let's kiss and make up!"
- **B.** "Don't have a cow!"
- **C.** "That's how the cookie crumbles!"
- **D.** "I'm just getting warmed up!"

Results:
Mostly As: Lippy Lips
Mostly Bs: Spilt Milk
Mostly Cs: Kooky Cookie
Mostly Ds: Toasty Pop

TROPICAL AISLE

There's nothing better than a tropical vacation to get the Shopkins' juices flowing. But now that their trip is over, they need help to get back home! Match the traveling Shopkin to the aisle he or she lives in.

A. Fruit & Veg
B. Party Foods
C. Health & Beauty
D. Pantry
E. Petkins

1C

2A

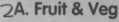

5E

3D

4B

JUST KICKIN' IT

When you step out with the Shopkins, you'll find they have style for miles and tons of sole. And they love to kick up their heels! Go toe-to-toe with them by drawing some of the coolest shoe styles you can imagine!

WRITE ON!

Turn the page to find some super-scrumptious story starters where YOU get to decide what happens to the Shopkins next! You'll also get ideas so you can write stories of your own . . . that are all about you!

FAIR WEATHERED FRIENDS

Lippy Lips couldn't remember a day as windy as this one. It was the perfect day to wrap herself in a fabulously stylish scarf and head to the park to try it out! But which one should she wear?

She had them in different shades for every mood. She wore her purple scarf when she was feeling pretty, her gray scarf when she was feeling sad, her lemon scarf when she was feeling silly, and her fuchsia scarf when she was feeling feisty. Today she was feeling happy so she chose a scarf in a perfectly lovely shade of turquoise. Nothing made Lippy happier than picking out an outfit!

She slung the scarf around her neck and looked into the mirror. It was going to be a beautiful day!

A day at the park was best spent with friends, so she called Toasty Pop, Apple Blossom, and Suzie Sundae, and asked them to meet her at the gazebo.

When she arrived, her friends were also decked out in their warmest, wooliest scarves.

"I love, love, LOVE windy days at the park," declared Toasty.

"Me, too," agreed Lippy. "It really opens up my outfit choices. But most of all, I love windy days because I can do this!"

Lippy began to pose and pout like the supermodel she dreamed of becoming one day. Her scarf flapped in the blustery breeze.

Suzie was impressed. "Okay, you're, like, uh-mazing in that scarf," she told Lippy.

Toasty and Apple agreed.

"Who doesn't love windy days at the park!" declared Apple Blossom.

Just then, a strong gust of wind blew something toward them. It was pink and round and . . . screaming?

"I HATE windy days at the paaaaaaark!"

Lippy grabbed the pink Shopkin. "Hold on tight, whoever you are!" she ordered.

"I'm June Balloon," the Shopkin replied as she grabbed Lippy's hand. June was happy to make some new friends. But she would be even happier if they could keep her from blowing away!

Toasty, Suzie, and Apple all greeted June cheerfully.

"I wish we could meet under less windy circumstances," said June.

Just then a strong gust of wind blew through the park, and Lippy lost her grip. The wind was mighty and June was light, and soon it was carrying her away!

"I'm sorry, June!" Lippy called. She would feel terrible if her new friend was hurt.

June floated high and low. She floated over the pond, through the gate, and out of the park. She floated so fast and so far that soon she was flying toward the Shopville plaza.

Lippy, Toasty, Suzie, and Apple hurried after her.

"OMG!" said Suzie. "She's headed toward the stationery store!"

"Oh, no! No! No!" said June. The stationery store was a dangerous place for a delicate Shopkin like June. It was full of all sorts of cute—but pointy—objects. "Too many thumbtacks. Too many thumbtacks!" she cried.

The Shopkins were all worried that June could pop! As that thought crossed Toasty's mind, a plan began to take shape.

Toasty began running toward the plaza at top speed. Suzie, Apple, and Lippy took off running behind her. But when Toasty was plugged into a good idea, she was hard to catch.

"Toast, coming in hot!" she yelled. With a flick of her levers, Toasty launched her toast slices into the air. She aimed them at the perfect height for June to catch. And when June had them safely in her arms, the slices worked like weights and helped bring June down to earth right in front of the stationery store steps.

"Thank you so much!" said June.

Her new friends looked exhausted. Exhausted, but happy! But as they huffed and puffed and tried to catch their breath, June started to lift back into the air.

What happens next? Turn the page to finish the story about what happens to June, and how her new friends Toasty Pop, Lippy Lips, Apple Blossom, and Suzie Sundae save her from unexpected surprises!

THE SHOW MUST GO ON

It's time for the annual Shopkins Talent Show! Lolli Poppins will play a few licks on the guitar and Tammy Tambourine is performing an original song. Le'Quorice will tell some sweet jokes—she likes black comedy—and Lola Rollerblade will do a skate routine. If you were joining the talent show, what would you do? Write about your hidden talents and special skills!

_____

_____

_____

_____

_____

X MARKS THE SHOP

"Arrrrrrr! What a day it be to sail the high seas in search of bounty!" cried the famous swashbuckler Captain Apple Blossom.

Okay, it was actually regular Apple Blossom. Apple and her friends were playing pirates. They were sailing through the dangerous waters of Shopville, bound for adventure. No one had ever seen a pirate ship as quick or as seaworthy as *The Salty Shopkin*, or a crew as loyal and true. Captain Blossom's crew included Cheeky Crossbones, Lippy Lafitte, and the first mate, Spilt Milk Sparrow. This was not their first voyage together. They had searched for sunken treasure, been stranded on tropical aisles, and even walked the plank. And together they were ready for anything that came their way, no matter how fresh . . . or how foul.

"What bounty are we in search of, Captain?" asked Spilt Milk Sparrow as the hot sun glinted off her golden hoop earrings.

"*Arrrrr*, Spilt matey!" Captain Blossom called. "The fabled treasure chest of Shop Island is what we seek." She pulled out an ancient-looking scroll and unrolled it for all her crew to see.

It was a treasure map! It was covered with images of strange sea monsters and lonely desert islands. A giant red X marked the spot where the treasure was buried. She lifted her eye patch and looked each member of her crew in the eyes. "A long time ago, an old sea dog by the name of Buccaneer Bud is rumored to have buried a chest full of mystical treasure. And we will be the first to find it!" Captain Blossom declared.

Cheeky, Lippy, and Spilt Milk all imagined how they'd look covered in diamonds and pearls and gold. The life of a pirate was hard, but there was always a silver lining—a reward of riches that would keep them sparkling for life!

Captain Blossom snapped her patch back into place, and lifted her spyglass to look out onto the sea. "But I wouldn't get too excited yet, me hearties. It looks mighty dark out there."

"Ay, Captain," said Cheeky.

"*Arrrrrrr!*" growled Captain Blossom.

Cheeky waved her hook to get the captain's attention. "No, I mean use your eye, Captain."

"*Arrrrrrr!* Of course," said Captain Blossom as she flipped her eye patch back up so she could look through her spyglass. She turned to her first mate and whispered, "How do you say 'thank you' in pirate?"

"Thank ye," offered Spilt Milk.

Captain Blossom turned back to Cheeky. "Thank ye, Cheeky Crossbones!" she said. She lifted her spyglass once again, and saw exactly what she'd hoped to see: Shop Island!

"There it be!" cried the captain. "Steer us to course!"

But before her crew could follow her command, a bunch of gigantic purple tentacles came bursting from the sea. They waved wildly to and fro, and eventually they surrounded *The Salty Shopkin*.

"Shiver me timbers!" cried Captain Blossom. "It be a creature from the depths of the sea! It be a . . . it be a . . ."

"Sea creature?" offered Spilt Milk.

"Yes, a sea creature!" yelled Captain Blossom. "All hands on deck!"

The sea creature's tentacles wrapped around the ship and began to drag it down toward the ocean floor. *The Salty Shopkin* was about to end up in the bottom of the ocean! How would they ever defeat the sea creature and make it to Shop Island to claim the treasure?

What happens next? *The Salty Shopkin* and its crew are in trouble, but they have a few tricks up their sleeves. Turn the page to finish the story about what happens to the crew. Can they overcome a monstrous sea creature? Will they find buried treasure, or be stranded at sea forever?

MOVIE MADNESS

The Shopkins love going to the movies. Soda Pops wants to see *The Wizard of Straws,* Dum Mee Mee is lining up for *Babe,* and Suzie Sundae can't wait to see *Ice Age.* What would a movie about your life be called? Who would it star? And what would happen? Now is your chance to tell an award-winning story . . . all about you!

_____

_____

_____

_____

SHOPPING CART RALLY

YOU could cut the tension in Shopville with a knife. It was time for the annual Shopping Cart Rally, and all the Shopkins were excited to see who would win!

From up in the announcer's booth, Apple Blossom and Kooky Cookie were ready for the big race to get underway.

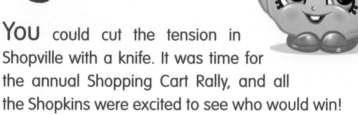

"Welcome to the Shopville Speedway," Apple Blossom said to the audience. "What a day it is to be racing! Perfect conditions on the track for our three competitors."

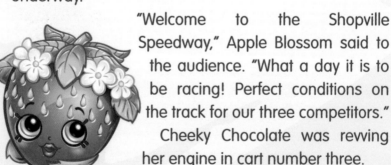

Cheeky Chocolate was revving her engine in cart number three.

Toasty Pop was ready to put the pedal to the metal in cart number two.

And Strawberry Kiss had her eye on the prize in cart number one.

"Who do you think is going to bring home the championship title?" Apple asked Kooky.

Kooky shrugged. All three Shopkins were great competitors, ripe with experience.

Apple grinned. "You're absolutely right, Kooky. Who knows who will win? It could be anyone's race!"

The carts idled at the starting line, and as the checkered flag waved, they rolled their way out of the gate.

"And they're off!" cried Apple Blossom.

Strawberry Kiss pulled ahead with an early lead, followed closely by Cheeky and Toasty as they blew through the Small Mart doors and entered Shopville.

But as they approached the stationery store, Strawberry took the first turn too fast and knocked a big eraser into the track. She managed to get out of its way just in time. Cheeky's cart rolled right over it, but Toasty wasn't so lucky. Her cart's wheel caught on the eraser, and as the tire spun, it began to smoke. The race was heating up!

"That's how you burn rubber!" Apple announced.

Now the carts were headed toward the fountain. They zoomed around it just in time to see that Spilt Milk was crossing the road. She saw the racers zooming toward her and skimmed out of the way . . . but not before leaving them an unpleasant surprise.

"Oh, no!" called Apple. "It looks like we have a slick on the track!"

Lead racer Strawberry didn't know what to do. There was nowhere to turn and she couldn't slow down. Her cart slipped on the milk slick and spun out of control, crashing into the curb.

"No, no, no, no, NO!" she cried.

Strawberry Kiss was out of the race and with two drivers left, things were getting juicy!

Too bad a second slick appeared on the racetrack. This one wasn't a spill at all. It was Slick Breadstick trying to get in on the racing action. But Toasty Pop and Cheeky Chocolate managed to avoid both slicks, and sped straight toward the Small Mart doors for the final lap.

Apple Blossom was on the edge of her seat. "Cheeky Chocolate moves into first place," she announced.

"What a race!"

Cheeky flew down the first aisle, with Toasty close behind. But Cheeky was reckless and blew through a soda pop display. The bottles tumbled into the track. Toasty swerved and spun, but she couldn't avoid them. One of them even landed right in her cart! Was she going to crash into the shelves and end her chances of taking the title?

"Looks like we need a cleanup in Aisle Three!" announced Apple Blossom.

Cheeky and Toasty sped around a corner, through the pantry, and headed for the checkout counter.

"What an amazing display of skill as our racers enter the final stretch!" cheered Apple.

As they zoomed toward the finish line, it was too close to call. Apple Blossom couldn't tell who would win the Shopping Cart Rally . . .

What happens next? Toasty and Cheeky are battling it out for first place. Turn the page to finish the story about who wins the Shopping Cart Rally . . . and bragging rights!

SUPER SHOPKINS SURPRISE!

It's D'Lish Donut's birthday, and the Shopkins are throwing her a sweet party! There will be presents, balloons, and party games—a recipe for success! But it's a surprise party, so don't spill the beans!

Who would you love to throw a surprise party for? Would the party have a theme? What music would you play? Write about the activities you would plan, the decorations you'd choose, and the party snacks you would have.

NO PAIN, NO GAIN

Cheeky Chocolate was getting ready for the run of her life. First, she put on her workout gear, including sweatbands for her wrists and forehead. Then she stretched out and got warmed up—not so warm she'd risk melting, of course! And now it was time for her training to begin.

She hopped up on the Small Mart register, turned on the conveyor belt, and began to jog. As she got into a sweet rhythm she cranked up the pace, and soon Cheeky was running faster than Lippy Lips on her way to a shoe sale. She ran and ran and ran, and then she ran some more. Cheeky had a goal, and would stop at nothing until she reached it!

"Hey, Cheeky!" Suzie Sundae, Toasty Pop, and Milk Bud stood near the register waving. Suzie's face was frozen in a confused expression.

"So, I don't want to alarm you, but I think, like maybe, you may be running in the wrong direction," said Suzie.

Cheeky just smiled. "I'm training for the Shopkins Olympics, Suzie! I'm going to be marathon champion of Shopville!" Cheeky imagined standing on top of a podium in a big stadium with a gold medal around her neck. All of the Shopkins would cheer her name and throw flowers at her feet. It was going to be sweet!

But Toasty Pop wasn't buying into Cheeky's fantasy. "Hey, I'm way faster than you, Cheeky," Toasty teased, laughing. "I can toast a bagel in ten seconds flat!"

"Uh, I don't know if that's, like, the same thing, Toasty," said Suzie.

"You think you can beat me?" Cheeky asked Toasty, smiling.

"Yeah!" said Toasty.

Cheeky Chocolate was ready for a fun challenge.

"Let's race!" she shouted.

It was going to be a battle for the ages. Cheeky, Toasty, and Milk Bud were set up and ready to race on register #1, #2, and #3. Suzie would be the referee.

"So, last Shopkin standing wins," Suzie told the runners. "On your mark, get set . . . OMG! Is that the newest issue of *Shopville Magazine*?" Suzie was easily distracted, especially when she saw a cover story about Slick Breadstick, the Baked Baron of Shopville.

Cheeky cleared her throat. "Suzie?" she called.

"Oh, yeah," Suzie said as she looked up from the story she was reading. "Uh, like, go!"

The racers took off running. Cheeky was barely breaking a sweat. She could stay fresh for hours! But Toasty wouldn't give up easily. She was practically electric with energy. Milk Bud wasn't much of a threat. He spent more time panting and licking his paws than he did focusing on the competition.

That gave Cheeky an idea. She grabbed a treat and tossed it toward her fellow racers. "Catch!" she yelled. The treat landed on Toasty's slices—but not before Milk Bud got a whiff of its meaty, doggie goodness.

"*Arf!* " Milk Bud barked. He didn't care much about the race—he just wanted that bone! He jumped up on Toasty, knocking her over and sending her tumbling down onto the register's conveyor belt.

"*Ahh!*" cried Toasty as Milk Bud ran into her. She didn't let this surprise keep her down for long. Once Milk Bud got his bone and hopped away happily, Toasty popped right back up and kept running. Nothing would stop her now!

What happens next? Now it's just Cheeky and Toasty in a race to the finish! Who will win? Who else is training to compete in the Shopkins Olympics? What other events are there? Tell the rest of the story here!

_____

_____

_____

_____

_____

SWEET DREAMS

The sun has set, the registers are off, and Small Mart is dark. It's bedtime in Shopville! Everyone is counting sheep, drifting off to sleep, and catching some ZZZs. Sweet dreams, Shopkins!

What's the best dream you've ever had? The scariest? What about the funniest? The weirdest? Write about the dreams you remember best!

_____

_____

_____

_____

FREE AS A STRAWBERRY

Strawberry Kiss wasn't the bravest Shopkin in the bunch. Even though she was a little afraid to fly, she'd always dreamt of soaring through the skies over Shopville.

So she was spending her afternoon doing the next best thing: making paper airplanes with Apple Blossom and Cheeky Chocolate at the stationery store in Shopville. The only problem was that Strawberry was rotten at folding the paper!

"Okay, Strawberry, let's try this again," said Apple Blossom hopefully. "You ready?"

"Ready," sighed Strawberry. She had spoiled the last

eight attempts, but she was determined to get it right this time.

Apple Blossom was a seasoned plane folder, and showed Strawberry what to do. She spoke very quickly. "Fold the paper in half, staple four times, hold this bit here, add some butter, fold that bit there, turn upside down, fold the wings down, bend the wing tips back up, do the hokey pokey and *voilà*! The perfect paper airplane. Easy!" explained Apple as she showed off her handiwork. Apple's paper airplane looked perfect. "Now your turn!" she told Strawberry.

Strawberry took a deep breath and set to work. "Fold the paper in half, staple two times, fold these bits there, dip it in butter, turn it around, then the bendy bits back, add some hokey pokey, and *voilà*?" She held up her creation for Apple's inspection.

Hmm, thought Apple Blossom. *That looks more like a crumpled bug than a paper plane.* "Uh, at least it has wings," she said.

"Coming through, guys!" called Cheeky as she tried to fit the world's largest paper airplane between

Strawberry and Apple. She'd been working hard on her plane to make it the fastest, strongest paper plane in history. If Cheeky's calculations were correct, this baby would fly higher than any plane she'd ever made before. Now she was ready to test it out. "Get ready for takeoff!" she said.

While Cheeky was launching her mega-plane into the wind, Strawberry was worrying about her plane's prospects. "I'll never get my plane in the sky," cried Strawberry as Cheeky's plane snuck up behind her. Suddenly, it slipped underneath her and glided into the air . . . with Strawberry on board!

Strawberry couldn't believe it. She was flying! And she wasn't sure she liked it. Her stomach felt like jelly!

"Apple, what do I do?" she shouted.

Apple's eyes got wide. "I know how to make them. I don't know how to fly them!" she replied.

Luckily, Cheeky was around to help. "Hold on to the sides," she told Strawberry. "And lean left or right to turn."

Strawberry tried to follow Cheeky's directions, and got the hang of it as her plane dipped down toward Shopville. She made a sharp turn just in time to avoid crashing into the stationery store.

"Nice work, Strawberry!" called Apple.

Strawberry felt so relieved! *Phew!* She sighed. Her plane flew into the air, kissed the clouds, and slowed as though it was floating on a summer's breeze.

But what goes up must come down. The plane took a nose dive. It hurtled faster and faster toward the big fountain in the center of Shopville. Strawberry tried to pull it up. She tried to steer left. She tried to turn right. But it was no use—the plane was going too fast, and Strawberry was about to become jam!

What happens next? How does Strawberry stop herself from crashing? Strawberry's amazing flying adventure is just beginning. Finish the story about where she flies next, what she sees, and how she makes it back home to Shopville!

_____

_____

_____

_____

_____

RAPPER'S DELIGHT

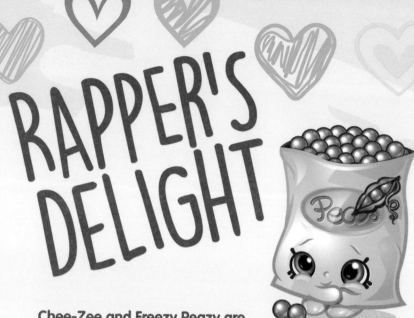

Chee-Zee and Freezy Peazy are feeling funky and fresh . . . and they've written a rap to prove it:

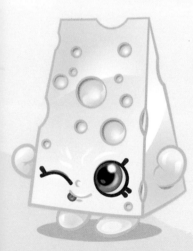

My name is Freezy and I play it cool.

This is my pal Chee-Zee and he ain't no fool.

We don't need to brag. We don't need to fight.

'Cause our beats are rockin' and our friendship is tight!

Now it's your turn! Write an original poem or rap about all the things you're good at. Then write one for your best friend!

_____

_____

_____

_____

_____

_____

_____

_____

_____

_____

_____

SHOPKIN HOLMES

It was a quiet day in Shopville—too quiet. It was the kind of day where something rotten was sure to walk through the doors at any minute.

Apple Blossom was playing detective, like the kind from a black-and-white movie. She wore a long overcoat and a hat pulled low over her worm, and flipped through the pages of the *Shopville Times* as she waited for a customer—any customer—to ask her for help.

As Shopkin Holmes, she was the finest detective Shopville had ever seen. With the help of her trusted sidekick Cheeky Watson, she had solved hundreds of cases around Shopville. Everyone knew they could trust her to get to the bottom of the stickiest situations.

But these days, business was slow. Shopkin Holmes had not had a new mystery to solve in days. She didn't really want anything bad to happen in Shopville, but she could not help wishing a new case would come along soon.

Just when she was about to give up all hope of anything interesting happening, a sweet-looking berry with a wild look in her eyes came bouncing into the office.

"Shopkin Holmes, we need your help!" cried Strawberry Kiss. "Kooky Cookie is . . . missing!"

This was exactly the kind of job Shopkin Holmes had been waiting for. She was on the case!

"Okay, where was the last place you saw Kooky?" Shopkin Holmes asked Strawberry.

"We were inside the Small Mart," replied Strawberry. Kooky and Strawberry had been doing some unapproved blueberry taste testing when Strawberry received a call from Lippy Lips. Strawberry had wandered off to see what Lippy wanted, and when she returned, Kooky was gone!

Shopkin Holmes smiled. If the facts were black-and-white, the Case of the Missing Cookie was going to be a slam dunk. She looked at her faithful sidekick and said, "Cheeky Watson, we have one hour to find Kooky...or it's too late!"

"Oh, no! Why's that?" Cheeky asked.

"I've got a dance class with Suzie at three," Shopkin Holmes said crisply. There was no time to lose. They needed to head to the Small Mart to look for clues at once!

When they arrived, they saw that the Small Mart was a total mess. There were blueberries and milk puddles all over the floor!

"I hope Kooky is okay," Strawberry said.

"Don't worry," Shopkin Holmes assured her. "We'll crack this case wide open. And we just got a step closer to solving it!" Shopkin Holmes had expert powers of observation and the giant puddles of milk were her first clue. She needed to interview the Shopkin who must have been at the scene of the crime: Spilt Milk!

They tracked the milk puddles, and when they finally found Spilt Milk, it took only seconds to get her to confess.

"Okay, it was me," said Spilt Milk.

"I knew it!" cried Shopkin Holmes. "So where is Kooky?"

"Huh?" Spilt Milk was confused. "I don't know where Kooky is. I thought you were talking about the mess." Spilt Milk had been walking through the Small Mart when she'd dripped, slipped, and tripped, sending milk and a display of blueberries flying all over!

"I ran away because I didn't want you guys to think I was so clumsy all of the time," Spilt Milk admitted.

Shopkin Holmes was puzzled. If Spilt Milk hadn't seen what happened to Kooky, their lead had run cold. "Then where on earth is Kooky?" she wondered.

What happens next? Kooky Cookie is still missing. But Shopkin Holmes is on the case. Finish the story about what clues turn up next, and how Shopkin Holmes finally tracks down her missing friend!

_____

_____

FUN IN THE SUN

One day, Cupcake Chic asks the Shopkins to give her ideas for a hot new vacation spot. Ice Cream Queen suggests a ski trip in the snowy mountains, while Melonie Pips gushes about the sunny beach. If you could travel anywhere in the world for vacation, where would you go? What would you do there? Who would you invite to come with you? Plan your dream vacation here!

_____

_____

_____

_____

A WALK IN THE PARK

One beautiful day in Shopville, Cheeky Chocolate and June Balloon decided to go on a walk through the park. As they strolled by the pond, they saw their friends enjoying the warm sunshine and the cool breeze. Everyone looked happy as clams. Everyone . . . except for Strawberry Kiss. She was dripping wet!

"Hey, Strawberry!" called June. "Did you fall in the pond again?

"No," said Strawberry. "But Milk Bud did."

To prove Strawberry's point, Milk Bud shook to dry himself off, and drops of pond water flew all over Strawberry once again.

Petkins like Milk Bud had tons of energy, but sometimes they were all paws! As Milk Bud continued to shake and shimmy and fling water droplets all over his friends, Apple Blossom came running over.

"Milk Bud!" called Apple Blossom. "I didn't mean that type of 'shake'!" She sighed loudly. "Sorry, Strawberry."

Cheeky looked confused. "What are you up to, Apple?" she asked.

"I'm teaching Milk Bud a few tricks," Apple explained. She patted Milk Bud on the head, and his tail began to wag furiously.

Apple decided to show her friends what Milk Bud had learned. "Milk Bud, shake," she commanded.

Milk Bud lifted a paw and put it in Apple Blossom's hand.

"Good boy, Milk Bud," said Apple Blossom. "You got the right 'shake' this time!"

Cheeky, June, and Strawberry were very impressed. "What else can he do?" asked Cheeky.

"He can do everything," said Apple. "Milk Bud, sit!"

she ordered.

Milk Bud sat.

"Roll over!" called Apple.

Milk Bud rolled over.

"Speak!" Apple declared.

Milk Bud began to bark happily. He loved learning new tricks! And Apple Blossom knew it. So she decided to show off the more advanced skills she'd been teaching Milk Bud.

"Speak French!" she commanded.

"*Bonjour,*" barked Milk Bud.

Apple and Milk Bud were just getting warmed up. "Make a balloon animal," Apple said.

Before June Balloon knew what hit her, Milk Bud began twisting and folding her into a balloon animal. She didn't mind, really, but it sure tickled. She hoped she wouldn't pop! Luckily, it seemed Milk Bud had learned this trick to perfection, too. Soon, June Balloon was a balloon kitten floating in the air!

Everyon cheered as June untwisted herself and drifted to the ground.

Now Apple Blossom had a really tough trick for Milk Bud to tackle. "Okay, Milk Bud," she said. "This is the true test." Apple turned to her audience. "There's another trick that we've tried only one time before. It was too hard for him at first—but look at all the amazing tricks he's done so far today! Maybe he finally has what it takes to pull it off!"

Milk Bud barked and began to jump up and down excitedly.

"Milk Bud," Apple Blossom called out loudly. "I want you to . . ."

What happens next? What truly amazing trick does Apple Blossom ask Milk Bud to do now? What else does Milk Bud do during his day at the park?

_____

_____

_____

_____

_____

_____

SHOPKINS FOR THE WIN

It's Field Day in Shopville, and all the Shopkins are getting ready to play some games. Breaky Crunch is going to box and bowl. D'Lish Donut is practicing her hole in one. Molly Mops is ready to mop the floor with the competition, but Poppy Corn is worried about being a real butterfingers! What kinds of games do you like to play? Are you on any sports teams? Write about the biggest match of your life!

This journal is a place to write, remember, and dream.
Fill in the rest of these pages with all of your sweetest
thoughts and tastiest adventures. Life is chock-full of
amazing things to check out and stories to dish about.
And with loyal friends like the Shopkins, you never know
what's in store!

HAPPY WRITING!

_____

_____

_____

_____

_____

_____

_____

_____

_____

_____

#APPLE_BLOSSOM

#D'LISH_DONUT

#KOOKY_COOKIE

#SNEAKY_WEDGE

SPK

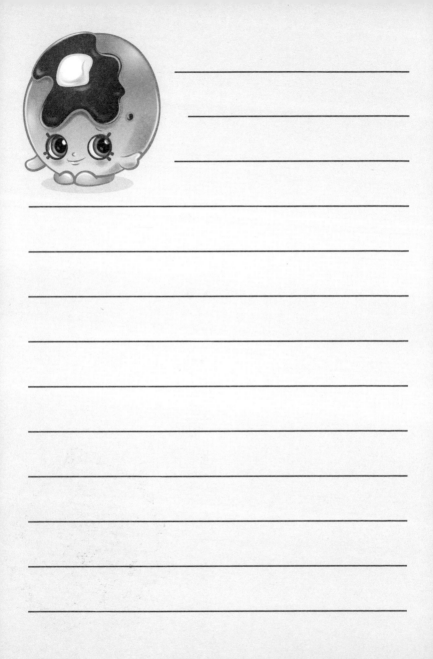

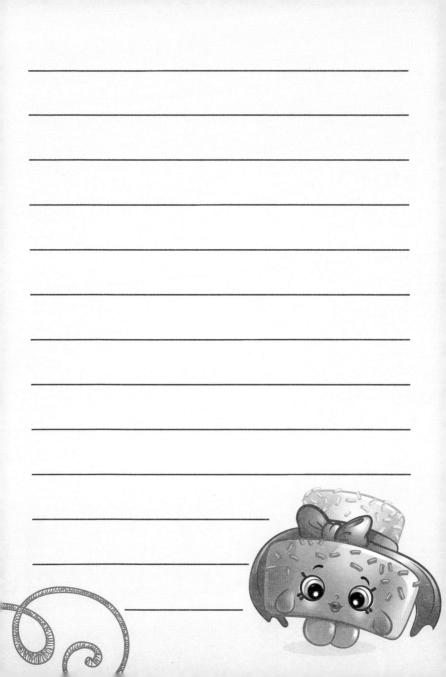

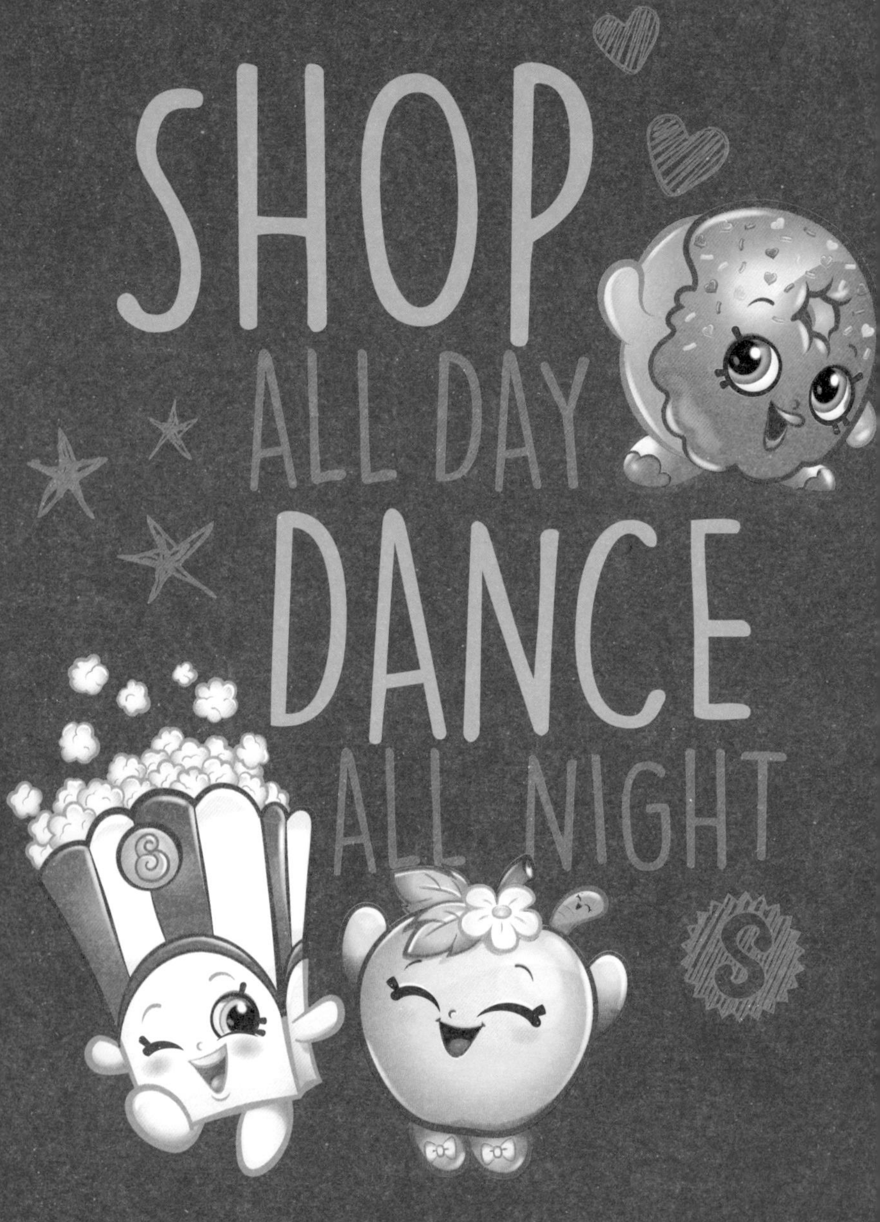
SHOP
ALL DAY
DANCE
ALL NIGHT

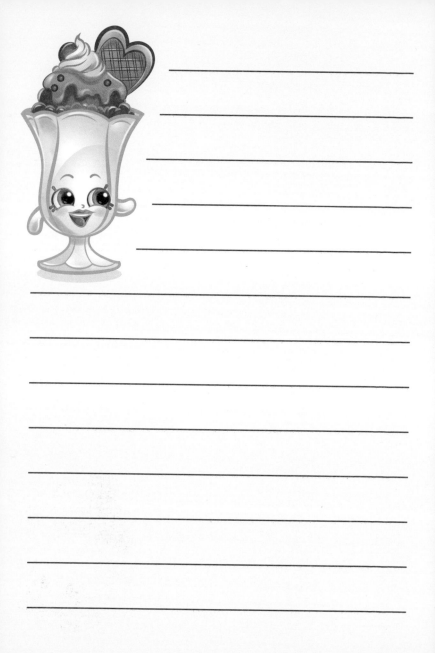

BEST FRIENDS FOREVER

Chloe Flower

D'Lish Donut

Bread Head

Yo-Chi

Freda Fern

**Mystery Shopkin:
Toasty Pop**

ANSWER KEY

THE GREAT SHOPKINS SEARCH

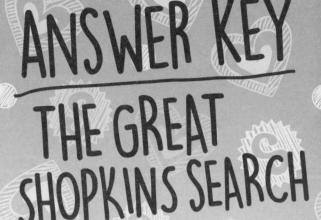

```
F  R  A  T  Q  S  C  A  N  T
R  M  P  O  S  C  H  A  B  O
E  I  D  A  F  T  L  N  O  A
D  L  I  S  H  D  O  N  U  T
A  M  B  T  G  A  E  R  I  Y
F  O  P  Y  L  S  F  B  C  S
E  N  Q  P  E  U  L  P  A  E
R  T  S  O  R  Y  O  C  H  I
N  J  A  P  F  P  W  B  A  G
B  R  E  A  D  H  E  A  D  I
F  L  U  Q  C  E  R  T  E  N
```